# THE WOUNDED BUZZARD
# ON CHRISTMAS EVE

John R. Erickson
Illustrations by Gerald L. Holmes

Maverick Books
Published by Gulf Publishing Company
Houston, Texas

This one is for Gerald Holmes and Trev Tevis, who have contributed so much to the Hank adventure.

Maverick Books
Published by Gulf Publishing Company
P.O. Box 2608 Houston, Texas 77252-2608

B    C    D    E    F    G    H

**Library of Congress Cataloging-in-Publication Data**

Erickson, John R., 1943–
    Hank the Cowdog: the wounded buzzard on Christmas
Eve/John R. Erickson; illustrations by Gerald L. Holmes.
        p.   cm.
    Summary: Accompanying Slim and Little Alfred into town on
a Christmas shopping trip, Hank and Drover run up against a
gang of toughs so mean and heartless, it's a wonder they ever
make it back to the ranch.
    ISBN 0-87719-176-X.—ISBN 0-87719-175-1 (pbk.).—ISBN
0-87719-179-4 (cassette)
    1. Dogs—Fiction. [1. Dogs—Fiction. 2. Christmas—Fiction.
3. West (U.S.)—Fiction. 4. Humorous stories.] I. Holmes,
Gerald L.; ill. II. Title.
PS3555.R428H35 1990
813'.54—dc20
[Fic]                                                        90-13564
                                                                CIP
                                                                 AC

Printed in the United States of America.

# Contents

**Have you read all of Hank's adventures?**
**Now available in paperback at $6.95:**

*All books are available on audio cassette too! ($15.95 for two cassettes)*

**Also available on cassettes: Hank the Cowdog's Greatest Hits!**

CHAPTER

# 1

# AN UNUSUALLY EXCITING FIRST CHAPTER, AS YOU'LL SEE

It's me again, Hank the Cowdog. You want to know all about the Wounded Buzzard, right? Such as his name and how he got wounded and other juicy morsels of the mystery? All in good time.

For the moment, let me set the scenery. It was a cold morning in December, the 24th of December to be exact, which just happened to be the day before Christmas—or, as we put it in the Security Business, "Christmas Eve."

Drover and I had come in from the night shift and were settling into our gunny sack beds, hoping to catch a little sleep and get a break from the grueling routine of ranch work, when all of a sudden we heard a car coming towards the house.

I leaped to my feet and began to bark. Whoever these trespassers were, they had no business on our ranch . . . only it wasn't a car.

Did you think it was a car? Not a bad guess, but it just happens that you're wrong. As I went sprinting out to challenge the trespassers, I began piecing together a profile of this strange vehicle that was uncroaching on my territory.

Clue #1: It had a flatbed in the back. Car's don't have flatbeds, see. They have back seats and back doors. That was my first clue that this was no ordinary car, but rather a *pickup*.

Clue #2: Lying upon and scattered about the flatbed were several items: a high-lift jack, a spare tire, several empty soda pop cans, a jumble of baling wire, and five or six empty gunny sacks. In other words, this alleged vehicle had all the markings of *a cowboy rig*.

Clue #3: But this was no ordinary cowboy's pickup, for you see, instead of having your usual telescoping radio ariel . . . errial . . . heirial . . . aireal . . . .

Instead of having the usual telescoping radio antenna, which would be standard on most ranch pickups, this one was equipped with *a special, highly sensitive radar antenna,* and we're talking about a top secret electronic device that could see in the dark and pick up small objects up to a mile away.

The next question was, "Who or whom would need that kind of sophisticated electronic surveillance gear in a pickup truck?" The answer was obvious. What we had here was a CATTLE RUSTLER who had equipped

G. L. Holmes

his pickup with highly sensitive, top secret, sophisticated radar equipment, capable of spotting cattle out in the pasture even in the dead of night.

Well, you know where I stand on the issue of cattle rustlers. If there's anything that gets me stirred up and brings out all of my in-bred cowdog instinks, it's cattle rustlers.

So it should come as no surprise that, while streaking out to intercept this villain, I not only barked but I put the entire ranch under Red Alert. That was a drastic measure I'll admit, but it had to be done.

The key to the whole thing was that radar antenna. That was the key to the lock to the door to the dark cellar of . . . it was definitely the key.

At first glance, that radar dish resembled an ordinary coat hanger that had been wired to the stump of the radio antenna, but that could very well have been a clever disguise calculated to throw children, fools, and dogs untrained in security work off the . . . .

Hold up. Cancel the Red Alert. Forget what I just said. Never mind.

Okay, what we had here was Slim driving his red, flatbed, four-wheel drive, Ford pickup into headquarters. Yes, I recognized the spare tire and the web of baling wire in the back end, and I remembered very clearly the day a bale of alfalfa hay had slipped off the top of the load and sheered off the radio antenna.

I also remembered very clearly that right after lunch that same day, Slim had wired a coat hanger onto the stump.

Okay. Drover had noticed none of this, of course, and now he was yipping his little head off.

"Save your breath, son, it's only Slim."

He stopped and squinted at the pickup, which had pulled up in front of the house. "Well I'll be derned. I thought you said we were under Red Alert."

"I said nothing of the sort. I said, 'Drover, this pickup is red. Be on the alert.' "

He sat down and scratched his ear. "Huh. How come we're supposed to be on the alert for red pickups?"

I walked over to him, shaking my head. "Drover, if you don't know the answer to that one by this time, I don't think it would do a lick of good to tell you." He licked his chops. I glared at him. "Why do you keep doing that?"

"Doing what?"

"Every time I use the word 'lick,' you lick your chops."

"I don't know. There's this little voice in my head that says, 'Drover, lick your chops.' And I lick my chops. It just seems the right thing to do, I guess."

"Well, it's NOT the right thing to do. It's inappropriate and irrational behavior. It's very much like a nervous twitch, and it makes you look silly."

Suddenly, his eyes twitched. "Oh my gosh, there's that voice again, and this time it said, 'Drover, twitch your eyes.' I can't help myself."

"Tell the voice to shut up."

"Shut up!"

"Watch your mouth, son, you're speaking to the Head of Ranch Security."

"I was talking to the voice."

"Oh."

"But it's still there, telling me to twitch my eyes."

"Very well, we'll have to go to sterner measures. What we have here is a clear case of compulsory behavior. Look into my eyes and repeat after me."

6

"Okay."

"Repeat: 'Voice of the mysterious twitch, voice of the irrational licking mechanism, away, away, be gone!' That should do it."

He tried it, and you'll never believe this, but it worked!

"Gosh, Hank, that sure did the trick. The voice is gone, my twitch has disappeared, I'm a free dog again!"

"Good. Excellent. I haven't used that trick in a long . . . ."

All at once, I heard this voice in my head—a still, small, high-pitched, rather whiney voice that reminded me of a certain obnoxious cat. And the voice said, "Hankie, twitch your eyes."

Drover was staring at me. "Did you just twitch your eyes?

"What? Twitch my . . . don't be absurd."

"There it goes again. Hank, I think you've caught my twitch."

"That's one of the most ridiculous things I've ever heard you say, Drover. There's no way that . . . ."

But you know what? I HAD caught his derned twitch, even though it was impossible. And, fellers, I had a pretty severe case of it. I

7

leaped into the air, scratched the side of my head, sprinted a short distance, and rolled in the snow.

And finally, the voice and the twitch went away. I stood up, shook myself, and returned to my assistant.

"Well, I licked that twitch." Now get this. His tongue shot out and swept across his chops, and his eyes began to twitch. "But I can already see that you're beyond help. You're a compulsory nincompoop, Drover, and you might as well accept it."

"Thanks, Hank. How come we're supposed to be on the alert for red pickups?"

"Red pickups? What are you . . . oh yes, red pickups. It's obvious, Drover, but if you wish, I'll give you a hint. "

"Yeah, that might help."

"In fact, I'll give you more than a hint. I'll give you the answer, and I'll expect you to remember it always. We must be on the alert for red pickups because fire trucks are red."

"Except for the tires."

"Hush. Fire trucks also drive very fast. Hence, any red pickup we see could very well be an emergency vehicle streaking toward the scene of a fire. We should be on the alert and give it the right of way. That's as clear as I can make it.''

"I still thought you said Red Alert.''

"I did NOT say anything about Red Alert. Just remember about the fire trucks, and if you have any further questions, don't hesitate to shut your little trap.''

Having completed Drover's lesson in Fire Truck Safety, I turned my attention to the yard gate. Slim was there, carrying a large box wrapped in red paper and crowned with a big green bow.

Obviously, this was no ordinary box. It had all the markings of a present. This being December, the month in which Christmas was scheduled to fall, the present could very easily have been a Christmas present.

The question was, for who or whom? I needed to check that out, for you see, although we dogs are not accustomed to receiving gifts and don't really expect to be recognized for the many services we perform on the ranch, a small possibility existed that Slim was bringing the gift for . . . well, for us.

Or, to narrow it down even more, for ME.

C H A P T E R

# 2

# A GIFT FOR ME?

I went padding up to Slim, just as he was going through the gate. I was glad to see the old rascal, and as you might expect, he was delighted to see me.

"Hi Hankie, what do you think of this snow?"

I jumped up on him and barked. He liked that. Things were definitely going my way, but just then a certain cat who had been loafing around on the front porch came streaking down the sidewalk.

I bristled and a growl began to rumble in my lower throat. "Scram, cat. This is my deal and you're not invited."

Would you believe it? Pete stuck out his tongue at me. "It's a free country, Hankie, and I can go wherever I want."

"Oh yeah?"

"And I want to say hello to Slim, and if you don't like it, just go sit on a tack."

"That's cute, Pete, and speaking of tacks, you're fixing to get yourself a full-scale attack that could land you in the hospital for about six months. In case you don't remember me, I'm the guy who doesn't take trash off the cats."

As he passed in front of me, he flicked his stupid tail in such a way that it tickled the end of my nose, causing me to sneeze. That sneeze was all that saved his life. Had I not been seized by a sneeze at that precise moment, I would have . . . you can guess what I might have done, but I didn't and couldn't because I had to sneeze.

And by that time, the cat had prissed his way on down the sidewalk and had begun rubbing up against Slim's legs. And purring. And grinning, just as though he and Slim were blossem buddies, which I happened to know they weren't.

To his credit, Slim ignored the cat and said to me, "Guess what I brought for you, old pup."

Oh ho! Yes sir, me and Slim had a good understanding and were the best of pals, and it was pretty clear by this time who was going to be the recipitant of that big lovely present.

He shouldn't have done it. I mean, these cowboys don't make much money, and any time they spend their hard-earned dollars on a gift, you know that they've made a sacrifice. And my opinion of Slim wouldn't have changed one bit if he'd skipped the present and just given me a pat on the head.

I mean, friendship—the real thing, the genuine article—begins in the heart, not in the pocketbook, and even though you can pick a friend's pocket, you can't pick his heart.

That doesn't make much sense.

On the other hand, the giving of gifts is a nice custom, especially when the receiver of the gift has proved that he deserves it, and if Slim wanted to reward me for a job well done, the least I could do was to accept it with grace. And humility.

Over the years, I have learned to accept good news as a legitimate part of life itself.

Slim set my package down in the snow and went back out the gate to his pickup, tripping over the cat on his first two steps. "Pete, get out of the way! You're worse than a boa constrictor."

Ho ho, hee hee, ha ha! I loved it. Slim was

my kind of cowboy. Not only did he buy expensive presents for the Head of Ranch Security, but he didn't like cats.

Well, there was my gift sitting right in front of me in the snow. Beautiful, gorgeous, red, shimmering, glistening paper, topped off with one of the biggest green bows I'd ever seen. Boy, was I honored and humbled!

Yeah, maybe he shouldn't have done it, but dern it all, I couldn't help believing in the warm deep cavities of my heart that he had put his money on a winner.

And just to be sure that Drover and Pete didn't get any strange ideas about whose present this was, I figgered it might be a good idea for me to put my mark on it, which I did.

You know, I'd marked a zillion tires in my career, but this was the first time I'd ever been given the opportunity—nay, the honor—of putting my mark on a Christmas present.

Just then, High Loper came out of the house and down the sidewalk, and Slim returned from the pickup. Loper glanced down at the present.

"What's that?"

Slim cracked a smile. "Oh, a little something for you."

HUH? Who?

"Merry Christmas, pardner. It ain't much, but for what you're payin' me, you don't deserve a whole heck of a lot." They both laughed at that. "And Hankie, here's your Christmas present. Merry Christmas, old pup."

And with that, Slim handed me a . . . AN OLD STEAK BONE? Surely there was some . . . I sniffed it, wagged my tail, gave him a look that I'm sure revealed the depths of my . . . .

"Well, if you don't want it, I'll give it to

15

Drover. Come here, Stub-tail, here's your Christmas from old Slim.''

Do you think Mr. Greedy turned it down? No sir. He snatched it out of Slim's fingers, darted a few feet away, turned his back on me, and began chewing and crunching and slurping and making other disgusting sounds.

Oh yes, and he even *growled,* as though he thought that I might lower myself to swagger over and take the bone away from him.

Which wasn't entirely out of the realm of possibility, but it happened that I was still so shocked and hurt over this other deal . . . oh well.

"Well, by gollies," said Loper, "I didn't expect you to get me anything." He picked up the present. "But since you did, I sure . . . ." He frowned, looked down at his hand, and wiped it on his jeans. "I appreciate it. Thanks."

"You're sure welcome."

"Only now," Loper said with a grin, "I guess you'll expect me to buy you something."

Slim rolled his eyes. "Well, that would be nice, and now that you mention it, I've been looking at that new A-fork saddle in Leonard's Saddle Shop and . . . ."

"Just keep lookin' and maybe old Sandy

Clothes will get it for you. I won't, but he might."

(Let me interrupt here to point out that this conversation, which appeared on the surface to be nothing but idle chatter between cowboys, gave me my first introduction to a certain character called 'Sandy Clothes.' At the time, the name meant nothing to me, but as you will see . . . well, you will see when it's time for you to see, and that's all I can reveal at this time.)

Slim dug his hands into his pockets and looked up at the gray sky. "You reckon you could handle the feed run today so's I can go into town and do a little last minute shoppin'?"

"Oh . . . I guess. 'Tis the season to be jolly and so forth."

Slim rocked up and down on his toes and kept looking up at the sky. "Well, that sure would be nice. It would be nicer yet if I had a little money to spend."

"Yeah, that money sure helps."

"Do you reckon . . . I thought maybe . . . ."

Loper grinned. "Oh. You don't want a paycheck or anything, do you?"

"Well . . . ."

Loper stuck two fingers into his shirt pocket

and pulled out a piece of green paper, folded in half. He handed it to Slim. "Don't spend it all in one place."

Just then, the front door opened and out came Little Alfred, Sally May and Loper's four-year-old boy. He was all dressed up in his red chaps and vest to match, a big felt hat, and a new pair of four-buckle galoshes over his boots.

All at once Loper's eyes lit up, and he turned back to Slim. "Say, I've got a deal for you, Slim. Why don't you take that boy with you and let him see the Sandy Clothes parade?"

(There's that name again.)

Old Slim's mouth dropped a couple of inches. "Well uh . . . ."

"He's all dressed and ready to go. He won't be any trouble."

"Well uh . . . ."

"He sure wants to go, but with me having to do all the feeding and everything . . . ."

"Yeah, well . . . ."

"I'd do your chores tonight, of course."

"Well, that might . . . ."

"And tomorrow, too."

"Tomorrow too, huh?"

"He sure had his heart set on seeing that parade."

"I'll bet he did. Oh, I reckon . . . ."

"Good deal!" Loper turned to the boy. "Alfred, Slim's volunteered to take you into town to see the big parade. What do you think of that?"

Alfred's face blossomed into a smile and he let out a yell. Slim looked down at me and muttered, "This *ain't* exactly what I had in mind for my day off."

Little Alfred raced down the sidewalk, flew out the gate, and stood at the door of Slim's pickup. The boy was ready to go to town.

Loper was all smiles. "Slim, you sure know how to make a boy happy."

"Yalp."

"Make him mind his manners."

"Yalp."

"See you around dark?"

"If we ain't in jail by then."

"Y'all have a big time." Loper turned to go back into the house, but then he stopped and scowled into the palm of his hand. "How did this present get so wet?"

"Snow, most likely."

Loper wiped his hand on his jeans and went back into the house.

CHAPTER

3

# A HEAD-ON COLLISION

S lim stuffed his hands into his jeans pockets and wandered out the gate to the pickup door, where Little Alfred was waiting. Slim's lips were pooched out and he had a scowl on his face. He looked down at the boy.

"Alfred, me and you need to reach an understanding right now. I want you to know that I'm pretty stern." Alfred nodded his head. "And going to town with me ain't likely to be as much fun as you might think." Alfred nodded. "And I've got things to do and I can't be chasing you around all day."

Alfred nodded. "I'll be good, Swim."

"You can do anything you want, as long as you don't move or make noise. I don't have much patience with kids."

"Okay, Swim."

"And don't forget," he shook his finger in the boy's face, "that I'm mean and gripey and no fun at all. And before you start asking for candy and gum and all that other stuff, the answer is NO."

"Okay, Swim."

"And the answer to everything else is NO."

"Okay, Swim."

"All right. Let's go to town."

"Swim, can we take my doggies to town wiff us?"

"Huh? DOGS? Them two dogs? Son, I wouldn't take them dogs with me to a dog fight."

"They'll be good."

"I'd be ashamed to be seen with 'em."

"I can play wiff my doggies while you shop."

"Absolutely, positively . . . ." Slim's gaze swung around to me. I whapped my tail in the snow and gave him my most innocent, best behaved look. "Come to think of it, that ain't such a . . . ." He turned his eyes on Mr. Ate-My-Bone, who was suddenly grinning and groveling and rolling around in the snow. "Well . . . maybe."

"Oh boy!"

"But they'll have to ride in the . . . ."

By then, Little Alfred had reached up and opened the pickup door. Taking this as my cue, I dashed out the gate and leaped up into the seat. Shucks, I was ready to go to town.

Oh yes, and Mr. Greedy scrambled in too, and sat his little self down on the seat beside me. I gave him a withering glare.

"You ate my bone."

"Was that yours?"

"Of course it was mine, you dunce. That was my Christmas present from Slim."

"Oh. I thought you didn't want it."

"Is that why you turned away from me and growled and slobbered and made all those disgusting sounds while you ate?"

"No, I was hungry."

"I've never been so embarrassed. All I can say is that you have no pride."

"Yeah, but I sure got the bone."

"That tells us a lot about your morals and values, doesn't it, Drover? You'd actually choose the momentary pleasure of a measly bone over the long-term satisfaction that comes from pride? Is that what you're saying?"

"Oh, it might depend on the size of the bone."

I looked him in the eyes. "Drover, I can't

tell you how disappointed I am in you."

"Good, 'cause I don't want to know."

"But for starters, let me say that you're a slob."

"Thanks, Hank, and it was a great bone."

At that moment, Little Alfred piled in beside us and slammed the door. Slim walked around the front of the pickup, shaking his head and talking to himself.

He got in, started the pickup, and off we went—up to the mail box, turned left on the county road, and headed for town.

He gripped the wheel in both hands and glared at the road ahead. Every now and then he'd let his eyes slip around to the three of us, perched there on the seat. He'd shake his head and say things under his breath that we couldn't hear.

When we crossed the third cattle guard on the way to town, he'd cheered up enough to say, "My first day off in two months and I get to babysit the boss's kid and two ignert dogs!"

Little Alfred sat in the seat between me and Mr. Bone Thief, with an arm throwed around each of us. "We'll have fun, won't we, Swim?"

"Boy howdy."

What happened next is kind of scary, so take

hold of something and I'll try to describe it just as it happened. You ready? Okay, here we go.

Suddenly there was a loud CRASH. The sound of broken glass. The squeal of brakes. Little Alfred screamed. Drover squeaked. Slim yelled, "Uh oh, hang on, y'all!" I don't know what I did or said, but very possibly I made an exclamation such as, "HUH?"

The pickup lurched from one side of the road to the other, went into a skid, bounced into the north ditch, and finally came to a stop. Then . . . silence. An eerie, unearthly, throbbing silence.

I ended up on the floorboard, with Drover on top of me and Little Alfred on top of him. "Drover, you're smashing me."

"Oh my leg!"

"Never mind your leg, you're smashing me!"

"What happened?"

"Never mind what happened, YOU'RE SMASHING ME!"

"I can't move, I think I'm paralyzed!"

It took a few seconds for my mind to clear. "Holy cats, Drover, we've had a wreck! It's coming clear now: the squeal of brakes, the sound of broken glass. Lie still. I think you're injured, possibly even paralyzed."

"I know."

"But you're still smashing me. Can you get off?"

"How can I move if I'm paralyzed?"

"I . . . that's a good point. See if you can wiggle your nose."

"Okay. I tried."

"And?"

"I can't see the end of my nose. Oh my gosh, Hank, I think my nose is cut off!"

"This is worse than I thought, but we mustn't panic."

"Wouldn't you panic if your nose was cut off?"

"The nose is gone, Drover, kiss it goodbye."

"I can't kiss it goodbye! My lips went with the nose!"

"No, what I mean is, accept the loss and go on with your life. Life without a nose is better than no nose at all."

"What will everybody say?"

"Oh, it won't be so bad, Drover. They'll probably say, 'Hey, look at that stupid-looking dog without a nose.' But you'll get used to it."

"Ohhhhhhh!"

"But the important thing right now is that YOU'RE SMASHING ME!"

"Is that all you can say to a dog who's been paralyzed and had his whole nose cut off?"

My situation had just about reached the critical point when suddenly it corrected itself. Little Alfred crawled off of Drover, and that provided a miracle cure for his so-called paralysis.

He moved, I scraped myself off the floorboard, and we found ourselves sitting face-to-face.

"Well, Drover, just as I suspected, you were not paralyzed and your nose is still where it was before."

"No, I think it moved."

"It did not move, you are not hurt, and therefore it follows from simple logic that you were smashing me for no good reason. Shame on you."

Just then, Slim spoke. And in speaking, he revealed for the first time the cause of our terrible accident. "Holy smokes, we just got a buzzard through the windshield!"

Four pairs of eyes turned toward a large feathered black THING lying in the seat. I sniffed it, checked it out, ran the sniffatory information through my data banks.

I turned to Drover. "It appears that we hit a druzzard, Bover."

"What?"

"I said, we hit a buzzard."

"Oh."

"That's what this dead buzzard is doing in the seat."

"Oh. I wondered. Gosh, is he really dead?"

"Very dead, Drover, but better him than us."

"I'll bet he doesn't think so."

"Dead buzzards don't think."

"Well, I guess it all worked out for the best."

"Exactly."

At that very moment, the dead buzzard flapped his wings and made a squawking noise, an indication that he wasn't as dead as he had first appeared. His wing, which was very large and powerful, struck me squarely on the nose, causing me to sneeze.

I sneezed.

Drover stared at me. "Gosh, you must be allergic to dead buzzards."

"He isn't dead, you moron."

"I thought you said he was."

"Never mind."

By time, Slim had opened his door and gotten out. He brushed the pieces of windshield glass off his coat and pulled Little Alfred

G.L.Holmes

outside and brushed him off too. Drover and I crawled out and shook ourselves.

Slim pushed his hat to the back of his head and looked in at the mess: the whole entire right side of the windshield was knocked out, the whole left side of the windshield was shattered and ready to fall out, the inside of the pickup was covered with what used to be the windshield, and a wounded buzzard was flopping around on the seat.

Slim heaved a big sigh and looked up at the sky, from which snowflakes were falling. "How do I get into deals like this—on my day off and the day before Christmas? Hit a danged buzzard!" He turned to Little Alfred. "Are you okay, Button?"

The boy nodded. "But the poor buzzood's hurt."

"Yeah, well, that's tough luck for the buzzard. My problem is that I've got to get to town and buy something for your momma and Miss Viola. Well . . . better clean up this mess and get back on the road."

He reached inside, gathered up the buzzard, set him down out in the pasture, and started sweeping the glass out of the pickup.

Up to this point, it hadn't occurred to me that I might know this particular buzzard. I mean, how many of us would claim to know a buzzard anyway? But then I heard a strange voice coming from somewhere in the sky above.

And the voice said, "*Oh my g-g-g-gosh, it's P-p-p-pa!*"

CHAPTER

4

# A MORAL DILEMMON: WHAT DO YOU DO WITH A WOUNDED BUZZARD?

As you may have already surmised, the voice I heard came from Junior the Buzzard.

As you also may have surmised, the alleged buzzard who had flown through and destroyed the windshield of Slim's pickup was Junior's old man, Wallace.

Whilst Slim was cleaning up the glass and feathers, Junior spiraled down from the sky and landed in the pasture beside his old man.

"Oh P-p-pa, s-s-s-speak to me, speak to me! Are you h-h-hurt b-b-b-b-b-b-b . . . terrible?"

Wallace was lying on his back, with his wings throwed out to the sides and his feet sticking up in the air. He lifted his head and blinked his eyes.

"Are you the gatekeeper of this place?"

"Uh . . . g-g-gate k-k-keeper?"

"You studder just like my boy Junior."

"I a-am your b-b-boy J-j-j-junior."

The old man squinted at him. "No you ain't. There's some resemblance, but you ain't Junior. He's down below."

"D-d-down below w-w-w-what, P-p-pa?"

"Down below, on earth. Do I have to pay to get in this place or is it free?"

"W-w-which place are y-y-you t-t-talking about, P-p-pa?"

"If you don't know which place you're at, who does? This here's Buzzard Heaven and I want in, even if I have to pay."

"N-n-no, this a-a-ain't B-b-buzzard H-heaven, P-p-pa."

"What! It ain't . . . in that case, mister, I ain't going in, and you ain't got horses enough to drag me!"

"B-b-but P-p-pa . . . ."

"Git away, don't you touch me, you buzzard devil!"

"B-b-but P-p-pa . . . ."

"Hyah! Sooey! Stand back, every one of you, before I have to tear this place apart!"

At that point, Junior gave up trying to talk to the old man and started waddling around in circles, shaking his head and saying, "Oh m-m-my p-p-poor P-p-p-pa! Oh m-m-my p-p-poor P-p-p-pa!"

Now, let me say right here that I'd never had much use for Old Man Wallace. He and I had run into each other on several occasions and he'd always struck me as a loud, overbearing, self-centered, unfriendly old buzzard.

But Junior was a different kind of bird. For one thing, he liked to sing, and anybody who likes to sing can't be entirely bad, even if he happens to be a buzzard. Junior had always treated me fair and square, and even though I didn't approve 100 percent of his profession and eating habits, I couldn't help liking him.

And it appeared to me that right now, he needed a friend. I mean, any time you find two buzzards and they ain't talking about food, something bad has happened. So I went over to him.

"Junior, I saw the whole thing and I know you must be feeling pretty bad right now."

"Oh m-m-my p-p-poor P-p-p-pa! Oh m-m-my p-p-poor P-p-p-pa!"

"Yes, he was a little slow on the take-off this morning and built a new window in that pickup there. It knocked him a little silly, appears to me."

"Oh m-m-my p-p-poor P-p-p-pa! Oh m-m-my p-p-poor P-p-p-pa!"

Junior was still hopping around in circles, repeating that same "poor Pa" business, and I couldn't see that it was doing either one of them much good.

"Hold it, Junior. Quit hopping around and listen to me." He quit. "You've got to get hold of yourself."

"B-b-but P-pa's h-hurt b-b-b-bad and t-t-talking c-c-crazy, and I d-d-don't know w-w-what to d-d-d-do."

"I know, Junior, that's what I mean. You've got to think this thing through and take it a step at a time. Now in the first place, your old man's had a wreck."

"I k-k-know."

"In the second place, he's hurt pretty bad. And in the third place, he might not pull through."

"Oh, d-d-d-don't s-say that! I w-w-wouldn't k-know what to d-d-do if a-anything was to h-h-h-h-h-happen to P-p-pa!"

"Yes, but you have to face it, Junior. It might come to that."

"Oh m-m-my p-p-poor P-p-p-pa! Oh m-m-my p-p-poor P-p-p-pa!"

"Now don't start that again. Hush up and listen." I sat down and put a paw on his shoulder. "The cold hard facts of the matter are that if your old man was a cat, a dog, a rabbit, a deer, a duck, or almost anything but a buzzard, somebody would come along this road, see him out there in the snow, take him home, and nurse him back to health.

"But Junior, there ain't many people in this old world who are shopping around for a wounded buzzard to take home. That's as plain as I can make it."

"Th-that's p-pretty p-p-p-plain."

"Which means that your old man might not pull through."

"Oh m-m-my p-p-poor P-p-p-pa!"

"And you have to prepare yourself for that."

"I c-c-can't d-do it!"

"Of course you can. Every coin has a silver lining, Junior. If Wallace doesn't make it, you'll be a free bird. You won't have to ask his permission every time you want to sneeze."

"If P-p-pa d-dies, I w-won't ever w-w-want to s-s-sneeze again."

"All right, forget sneezing. You can sleep late if you want. You can sing at all hours of the day or night. If you don't want to fly around looking for dead rabbits on the highways, you won't have to.

"Y-yeah, but I'd s-s-starve w-w-without P-p-pa."

"No you wouldn't. You'd adjust, you'd find a way to get by. I'm sure this kind of thing happens to buzzards all the time."

"W-w-well, m-m-maybe."

"Think about it, Junior. Hope for the best, but prepare yourself for the worst."

"O-okay, th-th-thanks."

With his head down and his wings drooped to the ground, Junior waddled off to himself, and while Drover and Little Alfred and I watched and listened, Junior sang this song.

My Daddy Had A Wreck Today

My daddy had a wreck today, I think it
    wrecked his mind.
He didn't have a lot to lose, what's lost,
    he'll never find.
My daddy's lying in the snow. He thinks
    he's somewhere new.

He's helpless, hopeless, all alone. I don't know what to do.

I'm thinking now of how he was, this morning on our roost.
He woke me up in the tone of voice to which I've gotten used.
He bellered, yelled, and fumed at me and said I'd never 'mount
To much of anything at all, I'm lazy and no-count.

If Pa should die and leave me here, I wonder what I'd do.
Spread my wings and fly away and start my life anew?
Or would I sit here in the snow and cry myself to sleep
And let the morning find us in one big feathered heap?

My daddy had a wreck today, I think I've had one too.
This rowdy partnership of ours is strange but also true.
I want my Pa, for good or bad, forever and a day.

And never mind my freedom, Pa, with you
   I'm going to stay.

The three of us listened to Junior's song, and by the time it was over, we all had some moisture in our eyes that didn't come from the snowflakes.

There to our left was Old Man Wallace, lying in the snow and babbling crazy things. And there to our right was Junior, the picture of a defeated buzzard.

Drover broke the silence. "Oh my gosh, that was the saddest song I ever heard! It just broke my heart."

Little Alfred sniffed and swiped at a tear that was running down his cheek.

Now, you must understand something about Little Alfred. He was still in that magic age when he could talk back and forth with animals. He could understand us and we could understand him. Whereas Slim hadn't heard a word of that buzzard's song, Little Alfred had heard it all.

And you could tell that it had punched him right in the heart bone.

"Poor old buzzood! Nobody wikes him. Nobody wants to help a poor old buzzood."

By this time, my mind was working at full

capacity, and in case you haven't been around a Head of Ranch Security when his mind is working at full capacity, I must tell you that it's very impressive.

My eyes moved from Junior to Wallace, then swung around to the south and locked on Slim, who was taking the last of the busted glass out of the windshield. Then I turned to Drover and Little Alfred.

"Boys, I think I've got this thing figgered out." And I told them my plan for saving Old Man Wallace.

Whether or not he *deserved* being saved was a horse with a different collar.

# 5

# I DISCOVER THREE MYSTERIOUS CAMELS

Slim had no idea what was in store for him when we went trooping back to the pickup. Little Alfred took the lead, I came along behind, and Drover rode the caboose, so to speak.

Slim had just removed the last section of shattered glass from the frame of the windshield and dropped it into a gunny sack.

"Well, there's that mess cleaned up. It's liable to be a little breezy driving to town against that north wind, but I bet we can do 'er. Load up, boys, we're burnin' daylight."

He threw the gunny sack full of glass onto the bed of the pickup and started to climb inside. It was then that he noticed us there—me and Drover sitting in the snow and wagging

41

our tails, and Little Alfred, our spokesman, holding his hands behind his back and looking up with big brown eyes.

Slim frowned at us. "What's this? Y'all want to go to town or sit on the bank and watch the crawdads eat? Let's go."

"Swim," Little Alfred began, "that buzzood's huut."

"Yeah, I noticed. He knocked a little chip out of my windshield. Load up."

"Swim, do you think . . . ." The boy rocked up on his toes and studied the sky. "Do you think we could take the buzzood wiff us and help him get well?"

Slim's mouth dropped open several inches. "Do I think . . . get well . . . a BUZZARD? Button, I've nursed sick calves and colts with distemper and baby rabbits and a couple of worthless dogs in my time, but I've never nursed a buzzard back to health." He shifted his chewing tobacco around to the other cheek and spit. "And I ain't fixin' to start now. Get in."

He got in and slammed the door. We didn't move. Little Alfred looked at me, and I looked at him and gave him the sign to move into Phase Two: Heavy Begs and Pleading.

Two big tears popped out of Alfred's eyes

and began rolling down his cheeks. At that same moment, Drover began to whine and I hopped up on my back legs and held the front ones out in the Beg Position.

Slim stared at us with a bewildered look in his eyes. "What is this? It wasn't my fault that a buzzard went through my windshield. He got just what he deserved."

Little Alfred squeezed out two more tears. Drover increased the volume of his whine. I held my begging paws higher.

Slim climbed out of the pickup, jerked off his hat, and slapped it against his leg. "NO! I ain't running a hospital for ruptured buzzards. My answer is no and no and HECK NO! Why, if any of the neighbors was to see me hauling a wounded buzzard around, I'd never hear the last of it. They'd laugh me plumb out of the county. No."

We turned up the volume.

Slim threw his hat on the ground and started waving his hands in the air. "Now, y'all stop that! I can't . . . nobody picks up wounded buzzards on the side of the road. It just ain't done! It ain't . . . I wouldn't know what to do with a derned buzzard if I had one!"

Again, we turned up the volume.

Slim stood there staring at us for a long time.

The hard lines in his face began to melt away. "I ain't believing this." He picked up his hat, shaped it, and slapped it back on his head. "If somebody had told me that I'd be . . . ."

All at once, he bent down and aimed a skinny finger at our spokesman. "Okay. But if you tell anybody that I did this, Little Alfred, and I'm talking about your daddy in particular—if you tell one living soul about this, I'll deny it. And then I'll tie a plow weight to your leg and throw you into the deepest hole on Wolf Creek!"

Our spokesman swallowed hard. "Okay, Swim."

"Okay." He snatched an empty gunny sack off the bed of the pickup, stomped out into the pasture, and began the process of gathering up Wallace the Buzzard.

That wasn't as easy as you might think. I mean, old Wallace was wounded and about half cockeyed, but he still had some fight left in him. He managed to squawk and flap and put up a pretty respectable struggle. One of his wings hit old Slim in the face, sent his hat flying and knocked his glasses down around his upper lip.

But Slim was no quitter. He got old Wallace caught by the feet and sacked him up. While all this was going on, Junior was about to have a stroke, hopping around in circles and squawking about his poor pa.

I slipped over and told him not to worry, his old man would get the best medical care available. To a buzzard, that is.

"We'll be down at Slim's place tonight," I said. "Check for us there."

Slim threw the gunny sack over his shoulder and walked back to the pickup. He found a loose cake string and tied the neck of the sack, so's Old Man Wallace wouldn't bust out on the way to town. He laid the sack, now filled with a wounded and crazy buzzard, right behind the cab.

Then he jammed his hands on his hips and scowled down at the three of us. "Now can we go to town? And can we make the trip without picking up any more strays and rejects? If I don't get my shopping done, my name's liable to be worse than mud."

"Wet's go to town!" cried Little Alfred, and all three of us piled into the pickup.

I had never been involved in such a trip before, where the trip was made in a pickup without a windshield and driving into a snow storm. We all liked to have froze to death, even though Slim had the heater running full blast. And by the time we made it to Waterhole 83 on the south edge of town, we had a fair-sized snowdrift started on the seat.

Slim stopped at the Waterhole, went inside and got himself a cup of hot coffee. Little Alfred didn't make a squeak or ask for anything. I guess he didn't want to push his luck.

While Slim was in the Waterhole, I glanced to my right and saw four town dogs sniffing at our tires. My first thought was to growl and tell the thugs to scram and leave our tires alone, and in fact, a growl did come to my throat.

But then . . . hmm. Hadn't I seen those guys before? Hadn't I once caught them on my ranch, whipped them, and run them off? Yes, indeed I had. Their names were Buster and Muggs, and there were two other hoodlums in their gang, whose names I didn't know.

They were tough guys, real tough guys. And I had reason to suspect that they didn't have fond memories of me. Hence, instead of creating a nasty scene, I . . . uh . . . scrunched down in the pickup, so to speak, and looked the other way.

There was no law against stray dogs, uh, checking out pickup tires at the Waterhole.

Slim came out, blowing on his coffee. He

kicked snow at the dogs and told them to scram, and I was sure that we would see no more of Buster and Muggs that day.

Little did I know . . . well, you'll see.

When Slim climbed back into the pickup, he pulled a candy bar and four pieces of bubblegum out of his pocket and gave them to Little Alfred.

"There, and don't you dare tell your ma that I bought you candy and junk."

Alfred was a pretty good boy—kind, unselfish, considerate of others, polite, had good manners—and he shared his candy bar with me and Drover.

Slim watched us swapping bites and curled his lip. "Boy, if your momma only knew . . . ."

We left the Waterhole, turned north, and headed into town on Main Street. Fellers, this was an exciting place! You've heard about New York and Paris and Amarillo? Well, those places may be bigger and a little fancier than Twitchell, but I can tell you that on the day before Christmas, Twitchell, Texas, is one of the most exciting places in the whole entire world.

I mean, they had cars and houses and stores and people and dogs, a big wide Main Street with candy canes and holly wreaths hanging from the light poles, colored lights strung across the street, people carrying packages out of stores, Christmas carols in the air—I mean, the whole nine yards of excitement.

Oh, and did I mention the camels? Strangest thing I ever saw. Three head of camels on the court house lawn! Also some sheep, two donkeys, a little barn, four or five guys standing around with rags on their heads, and . . . a BABY?

Now, I've told a windy tale or two in my life, but this is the whole absolute truth. They all stood there motionless in the cold and the snow, didn't move a whisker or an eyebrow the whole time I watched them.

Oh, and they weren't wearing coats either.

Don't ask me what camels were doing on the court house lawn, but I saw 'em there.

Anyways, Twitchell was a very exciting and mysterious place, and to a dog fresh off the ranch it was almost, by George, overwhelming.

Slim motored down the street, squinting at the stores and saying their names. Every now and then he'd find that the pickup had wandered across the center line and he'd jerk it back over.

At last, he found the place he'd been looking for. "There we go! Foxie's Ladies Wear. That's the place for me."

He herded the pickup into the nearest parking place against the curb, and we began our adventures in town.

Lots of adventures, but we didn't see any more camels.

# 6

# THE POODLE INCIDENT

We climbed out of the pickup. I looked down the street at all the cars parked against the curb.

"Holy smokes, Drover, we've got to mark all these tires before we leave."

"Oh my gosh. It tires me out just to think about it."

"I know what you mean, but it's got to be done."

"How come?"

I glared at him. "What do you mean, *how come?* Do I have to explain everything to you?"

"Well, not everything, but how come we have to mark tires in town? Aren't we off duty?"

Hmmmm. I really hadn't thought that one

out to its logical extremities, but . . . I had this powerful instink, see. It kept telling me that a good ranch dog shouldn't rest until he had marked every tire in sight.

That worked okay out at the ranch where the traffic wasn't too heavy, but here in this huge town with cars lined up by the dozens . . . a guy could work himself to death.

In other words, for the first time in years Drover had raised an important question: Why should a ranch dog feel a mortal obligation to mark every tire in town?

"Tell you what, Drover, let's mark three or four apiece and call it good. That's close enough for government work."

"What does that mean?"

"I don't know what it means, but that's what Slim says every time he builds fence, and if it's good enough for Slim, by George, it's good enough for me. Come on. I'll take the first one and you take the second."

We threw ourselves into the task and had just about notched up our four or five apiece when Slim saw us and called us back.

"Hank, cut that out! Come back here." We went over to him, sat down, and wagged our tails. "Quit acting like a couple of country fools. You're in town and there's ladies around, so mind your manners.''

He shifted his eyes to Alfred. ''Now, I'm going into this store to Christmas shop. You stay here close and make these dogs behave, or I'll take all three of you to the dog pound.''

''Okay, Swim, we'll be vewy, vewy good.''

Slim grunted and checked to be sure the buzzard was still tied up in his sack. Then he adjusted his hat, slapped some mud off his pant legs, took a deep breath, and plunged into Foxie's Ladies Wear, saying, ''Well, here's goes,'' under his breath.

About a minute later, he came back out, unloaded his chewing tobacco, and pitched it into the gutter.

The three of us sat down on the curb and waited and concentrated extra hard on being good. The first minute went by pretty fast, but after that the time sure began to drag.

I hate sitting around. Waiting. Doing nothing. Burning daylight. Killing time.

Fellers, I was bored. I got up from the curb and began pacing around. Back and forth, back and forth. But with each circle, my backs and forths got a little further apart until I had strayed, so to speak, from the sidewalk immediately in front of Foxie's Ladies Wear.

I had reached the north end of my pacing perimeter and was about to turn back south, when all at once I heard a sound that caused my paws to stop in their tracks.

I lifted my head, raised my ears to Semi-Alert position, and listened. Barking? Yes, barking, and it appeared to be coming from inside a certain big white fancy car parked at the curb nearby.

The barking was high-pitched and shrill, and I noted a certain insulting tone about it. I listened more closely and began to desiphon the message. What I had originally thought were mere sounds began to take on the shape of words: "Yee yee yee, you can't touch me! Har har har, I'm safe in the car! Ho ho ho, you're out in the snow!"

It was then that I noticed the little white poodle sitting up on top of the seat in the big white car. I glanced around to see if perhaps he had been directing his smart remarks at someone else. Seeing no one else nearby, I swaggered over to the car.

The window was open a crack on the driver's side. As I approached, the poodle went into a frenzy of barking—yapping, actually, since poodles don't have whatever it takes to make a decent barking sound. All they can do is yap and yip.

He yapped and yipped, and by the time I hopped up on my back legs and looked in the window he was lunging at me and talking all kinds of trash.

"You'd just better get your nasty paws off my car!"

"Excuse me," I said, "but I thought I heard somebody over here making some smart-mouth remarks. I don't suppose you'd know who that was, would you?"

I noticed that his hair was all clipped and shaped. He was wearing a rhinestone collar around his neck, and his toenails were painted. That was a new one on me—painted toenails.

"It's a free country," he said, "and I can say anything I want to say, and what I want to say is yee, yee, yee! And if you don't like it, just come through that window and see what happens."

I studied the opening and saw that it was about three inches wide. "You know, if you'd drop that winder another six inches, I'd sure do my best to get in there with you."

"You'd be sorry if you did. I'd tear you up so bad, you'd think you'd picked a fight with a chain saw."

"Oh yeah? I'll take my chances. Go ahead and drop that winder."

He yipped and yapped. "I think you're chicken. I think you're scared to death of me, and you're just lucky there's a window between us, otherwise . . . ."

"Otherwise, Mister Smartie Mouth, I'd make trotline bait out of you in about fifteen seconds—if I could catch you, that is, which I doubt that I could."

"Oh, you're a big talker, aren't you? Huh? Huh? You just come through that window and see what happens! Come on, I dare you!"

I hate getting involved in childish . . . on the other hand, a guy has to defend his honor. "Okay, we'll just see what I can do."

The poodle stopped yipping. His eyes got real big. "Don't you dare . . . you'd just better not, I'll call for help, I'm warning you!"

I knew I couldn't jump through the window, but I couldn't resist giving the little shrimp a scare. I leaped into the air, and at the top of my jump I wedged my mouth and enormous jaws through the crack and made some ferocious sounds that I figgered would give the pipsqueak a thrill.

It did. He went screaming to the other side of the car seat. I mean, the way he was hollering, you'd have thought I'd tore off one of his legs.

"Help, help, murder! He struck me, he bit me, he's trying to kill me!"

This was turning out to be more fun than I'd expected, certainly better than loafing around on the curb. I kept it up, even added a few new sounds to give him an extra . . . WHAP!

Huh?

G.L. Holmes

Unless I was badly mistaken, something had struck me on top of the head and knocked me to the street. I looked up, shook the checkers and stars out of my head, and saw the lady's handbag just before it struck me another blow. WHAP!

"You leave Foo Foo alone, you big nasty bully! The very idea! You've scared the poor thing half to death."

Well, hey, her sweet little Foo Foo had . . . WHOP! Trying to explain things to crazy women has never . . . WHOP! Seemed a pretty good time for me to sell out and find a better climate.

I think she had two rolls of quarters in that handbag.

I shot the gap between her legs and made for the sidewalk. It was my good fortune that Slim had just come out of the store, so I made a dash for him and took cover behind his legs.

He hadn't seen the woman. He'd just fished into his shirt pocket for a fresh chew when she marched up to him and whopped him on the shoulder with her bag.

"There, take that, you ruffian! You ought to be ashamed of yourself, letting your big oaf of a dog terrorize my poor little Foo Foo!"

"Whaaa . . . ?"

"You've ruined his Christmas, he's a nervous wreck, he won't be the same for weeks, oh, I'm SO UPSET, I think I'll hit you again!"

"Now hold on a . . . ." WHOP!

"Furthermore, I'm going to report this to the police, and I'm half a mind to consult my attorney, but before I do I'm going to hit you again!"

"No, I don't think you will," said Slim. She swung and this time he dodged, caught her by both shoulders, spun her around, and marched her towards the car door. "Get in the car, ma'am, before you fall and break your neck."

She let out a gasp. "Don't you DARE break my neck! We have laws in this town, and you'll be hearing from my attorney. You, sir, are no gentleman."

"Thank you, ma'am."

"You, sir, are a bully and a bully!"

"Yes ma'am."

"And my attorney will be in touch!"

She plunged into the car, scooped up little Foo Foo in her arms, kissed his face, gave us one last killing glare, and roared out of the parking space.

We watched her go squealing down Main Street. Slim took a bite off his chew and looked down at me. I, uh, whapped my tail on the sidewalk and squeezed up a smile.

"Thanks a bunch, Hank. After taking a buzzard through the windshield, what I really needed was to get attacked on the street by some poodle's mommie, the old rip."

He heaved a sigh. "Merry Christmas, baloney. It don't take me long to get my fill of Christmas shoppin'. You can't buy anything in that derned store unless you know some sizes. How's a guy supposed to know sizes? Walk up to a lady and put a tape measure on her? I can see me doin' that . . . and then picking up my teeth off the floor."

We stood there for a long time, watching the cars go down the street. "Well, let's wander down to the saddle shop. If I'm going to be arrested and throwed in jail, I'd just as soon be amongst friends."

He called to Drover and Little Alfred, and the four of us hiked half a block north to Leonard's Saddle Shop. Along the way, Slim reached down and scratched me behind the ears.

"You ain't much of a dog, Hank, but I'm sure glad you ain't a Foo Foo."

Say, that made me proud! I held my head and tail high in the air and marched a few steps out in front of everyone else. In this old life, a dog takes the roses as they come, even if they are a little wilted.

# LEONARD'S SADDLE SHOP

I was the first to arrive at the door of Leonard's Saddle Shop, and when I looked through the glass, I saw a big friendly gas stove over near the south wall.

It was cold outside on the street. Very cold. Even though I was accustomed to roughing it, sleeping in the snow, taking the very worst that Nature could throw at me and laughing it off as if it were . . . I was not unmindful of just how pleasant life in front of a gas stove could be.

Of course there's a price for all these luxuries. I was aware of that, too. A dog can get used to the easy life and it can sure ruin him for the . . . .

But on the other hand, there was a nice

friendly stove and, what the heck, when Slim pushed open the door, ringing the cowbell that hung above it, I squirted through his legs and made a dash for the stove.

Drover was only a few steps behind me. We curled up in front of the stove and showed through our actions and outward signs that we would be models of good behavior, if only we could stay inside by the stove.

Leonard, the guy who ran the place, was back in the shop driving wooden pegs into the sole of a boot. He looked at me and Drover over the tops of his glasses, then he turned to Slim and smiled.

"Well, lookie here what's walked into my store! One broke cowboy, two fine ranch dogs, and an urchin child, and I'll bet all four of you couldn't scrape together the price of a cup of coffee. I might as well lock the door and close up for the holidays."

Slim chuckled at that. "Leonard, I'll throw them dogs outside if you don't want 'em in here."

Leonard laid down his hammer, wiped his hands on his apron, and came out to the counter. "No, they're fine. I never wanted to work in a place where a dog wasn't welcome. If it ever comes to that, I'll close the doors and go back to cowboying. Besides, them's bound to be high-dollar cowdogs.''

I whapped my tail against the wood floor. Leonard was a pretty sharp judge of dogs, I could see that right away.

Slim laughed. ''They EAT high-dollar, but they WORK low-peso. Old Hank there just got me whupped on the street by a mad old woman.''

He told the story about the poodle, and Leonard got a big kick out of it. Then Slim told him the story about running into the buzzard, and Leonard doubled up and slapped his knees.

''Say, Slim, you've just about gone through your good luck and started on the bad, sounds to me like.''

''And I've still got to buy Christmas presents for two ladies, and I'll just be derned if I know what to get. I prowled around in Foxie's and didn't see one thing that didn't cost too much, embarrass me to ask about, or need a size. And I'm runnin' out of time.''

Leonard's eyebrows rose. He licked his lips. ''You got any money?''

''Oh sure. I just drawed my two-weeks wages.''

''Uh huh! Well now, this is your lucky day

and you have come to the right place."

"What do you mean?"

Leonard hitched up his pants and laid his hand on Slim's shoulder. "You have stumbled into a store that is famous for its Christmas gifts for ladies."

"Aw heck."

"It's true, honest, cross my heart. I wouldn't fib to an old cowboy friend. Just tell me who you're buying for."

"Well . . . Miss Viola and Sally May, but . . . ."

"Perfect! Would you believe that this very week those same two ladies, and I mean both of 'em, were in this very store?"

Slim reached under his hat and scratched his head. "Well, it don't sound exactly . . . ."

"Yes sir, in this very store, just a-gushing over all my beautiful stuff and wishing they had some of it."

"I'll be derned. Like what?"

"Well, let me think here." Leonard tugged on his chin and looked up at the ceiling. "It was Monday that Viola come in here, and what was she looking at?" He snapped his fingers. "Yes! She was looking at these five-buckle overshoes, come right on over here, Slim, you'll love these overshoes, just got 'em in, new shipment, and they've been selling like crazy, and mostly to the ladies.''

"I wouldn't have thought . . . ."

He led Slim over to the overshoe department, and pushed a boot into his hands. "Now Slim, *that is an overshoe.* Look at them buckles. Good rubber, tough, you won't tear out that boot.''

Slim looked it over and nodded his head. "That's a good overshoe, all right, but somehow . . . this is for Christmas, Leonard.''

Leonard stared at him. "You don't think Viola would be surprised and delighted and as pleased as punch if you gave her this great pair of overshoes?''

"Well, to be truthful about it . . . ."

"And she'll never know about the special deal I'm going to make you.''

"What special deal?''

"Our special Cowboy Christmas Deal. Now come on over here." Leonard took him by the arm and led him over to the bridle reins. "As I recall, Sally May was looking pretty serious at these new bridle reins. Look how thick they are. Son, *those are bridle reins.* Six feet long, cut out of the center of the hide, nothing cheap about these. Take 'em in your hand and feel of 'em.''

Slim took hold of them and nodded his head. "Good reins, all right, but Leonard, she don't have too much chance to ride these days now that she's had that baby."

Leonard raised a finger in the air. "That's right, she said that, I remember now, and that's when she moved over—come on over here, let me show you what else she was looking at." He took a long yellow rain slicker off a peg and held it out. "Slim, I thought that woman was going to carry this off, she was so crazy about it."

"A slicker? What in the world would she . . . ."

"Hey, she helps with the ranch work. She's got chickens to feed and eggs to gather and children to chase all over the ranch. Would you want that poor honest hard-working mother to go out into a storm without a decent slicker?"

"Well . . . ."

"Of course not! And once again, she'll never know what a great price I gave you, or . . . ," Leonard dropped his voice and glanced over his shoulder, "or that I sweetened the deal by throwing in a pair of boots—for you!"

Slim's expression changed all of a sudden. "Pair of boots, huh?"

"Slim, how long has it been since you bought yourself a new pair of boots?"

"Well, let's see . . . ."

"And I'm not talking about those old rough bullhide work boots. I'm talking about a REAL pair of boots, the kind that every cowboy dreams about? Years, right? Maybe never. Okay, step right over here."

"Now Leonard, you're moving kind of fast for me and . . . ."

Leonard picked up a new boot and held it up. "Slim, this is the boot you've always dreamed of owning but never allowed yourself to buy because, well, you're kind of cheap, and your really fine boots do cost a little money, but are they worth it? You bet your life they're worth it!

"This boot was made for you, Slim. Look at it, feast your eyes on it. That's genuine elephant ear. Tough? You can't wear it out. And it's got the toe you like and your kind of heel."

"Well, it is . . . ."

"Let's see, you wear a 10 D, right?"

"Uh . . . nine and a half B, I think."

"You'll want a 10 D in this boot—here, slip it on." He pushed Slim into a chair and pulled off his right boot. "Whoa, mercy! Son, something has crawled up and died inside your boot! See, that's what happens when you wear your boots too long. They get to stinkin' and it's time for a new pair. Stand up. How does that feel?"

"Well . . . ."

"Didn't I tell you that would be the best boot you ever stuck your foot into? Slip on that other one and walk around. I want you to be sure they're perfect for you."

"Well, it does feel pretty good, and I guess . . . ."

Slim pulled on the other boot and walked around in front of the mirror. While he was doing that, Leonard scratched some numbers down on a piece of paper.

"What do you think now?"

"I like 'em, I sure do."

Leonard flashed a smile. "I thought you would. Now Slim, them boots list for 400 dollars."

"Holy cow, get me out of these things!"

"BUT . . . I promised you a special deal, right?"

"It'd have to be real special."

"We're talking a package deal: overshoes, slicker, and boots—no more shopping around for the ladies, you can head back to the ranch and take care of that wounded buzzard, ha! How much is that check for?''

"Well, I don't know, didn't look.'' Slim rummaged through his shirt pocket until he found the check. "It's for $237.58, that's with Social Security taken out.''

Leonard's face went blank. "$237.58! Whoa! There's no way I can let all that stuff leave my store for that price.'' Slim shrugged and started to pull off the boots. "BUT . . . we can sure set up the balance on monthly payments.''

"Uh uh. Me and monthly payments don't get along.''

Leonard threw up his hands and shook his head. "All right, okay, keep the dadgum boots, take it all, it's Christmas and what the heck, a deal's a deal. Endorse that check and get out of here before I break down and cry.''

Leonard watched while Slim wrote his name on the back of the check, then he snatched it away. "Now Slim, if you ever tell my wife or my banker I did this, I'll have to call you a liar.''

"Well . . . .''

"Here's your stuff.'' Leonard boxed up Slim's old boots and pitched him the box. Then he added the overshoes and slicker to the pile in his arms. "You're a shrewd man, Slim, too shrewd for me. It's a good thing you don't come in here more often. I'd be out of business."

"Actually, I wanted to look at your ropes."

"Ropes? You got any money left?"

"No, you got it all."

"Son, you don't need a rope, it would just get you into trouble." He began easing Slim toward the door. "Besides, you need to get along home and take care of that wounded buzzard—that was a great story—and I'm going to close up shop and start the holiday." He opened the door. "Merry Christmas, you old rascal."

"Merry Christmas, Leonard. Come on, Button."

Drover and I were still soaking up the warmth of the stove. We weren't quite ready to leave, see. Leonard came towards us.

"Time to leave, doggies," he said with a smile. Then the smile slipped and he said under his breath, "Get out of here, you idiots."

We left the store and joined Slim out on the sidewalk. He was standing there with his armload of presents, watching the snowflakes come down.

"Well," he sighed, "broke again. I sure hope Miss Viola likes her galoshes."

Behind us, Leonard locked the door, drew the blinds, and turned off the light.

# 8

# DROVER SNAPS AT SNOWFLAKES

We made our way back down Main Street. Now and then we caught the sound of Christmas music coming out of the stores we passed. Ahead of us, whisps of snow swirled along the sidewalk.

Little Alfred began tugging on Slim's pantleg. "Swim, I want to see the Santie Cwaus pawade."

"Huh? Oh yeah, I almost forgot the parade. No, we wouldn't want to miss that, would we? Although . . . son, didn't you see Santie Claus last year?" The boy nodded. "Well, it's about the same every year. You might rather go home, what do you think?"

"I want to see the pawade."

"Sure you do, but you look kind of tired and

73

wore out, all this walkin' around and shoppin' and stuff, and we could sure put it off until next year."

"I want to see the pawade."

"You ain't tired?"

"No."

"You ain't cold?"

"No."

"You ain't hungry?"

Alfred's eyes brightened. "Can we get a hamboogoo?"

"I'm broke, son, been picked as clean as a goose. But I'll bet your momma has a big pot of stew on the stove back home."

He shook his head. "I want to see the pawade."

"You want to see the parade. Well, in that case I guess we'd better stay and see the parade. On my tombstone they're gonna put, 'Slim never could hold on to a dollar bill, but he was always nice to dogs and children.' What time you reckon this parade is liable to start?"

Little Alfred shrugged. "Fifteen o'clock, I think."

Slim smiled at that. Then his glance fell on the store in front of which we were standing, and his eyes brightened. "My, my, lookie where we are. Tell you what let's do, fellers. I'll run in here for a second and ask about that parade. Button, you take the dogs and wait for me at the pickup."

"Okay, Swim, but huhwee up."

"Oh, I won't be long. Y'all be good and stay out of mischief, hear? See you in a few minutes."

And with that, he walked into the store. When he opened the door we heard the sounds of men's voices, followed by a loud CRACK. The sign on the front window of the store said, "Pool Hall."

"What's a pool hall?" Drover asked.

"It's a big hall with a pool at one end."

"A pool of what?"

"Water, of course. What else would you find in a pool?"

"I don't know. You think he's going to swim?"

"Well, I sure hope he swims. If he doesn't, he's liable to drown. Those pools can be pretty deep."

"Gosh, I wouldn't want to go swimming in this cold weather."

"That's good, Drover, because nobody invited you to swim. You were invited to stay at the pickup."

"That's fine with me. I hate water anyway, especially in the winter."

We left the front of the swimming pool and wandered on down the street. Slim's pickup was parked at the curb a short ways down. Little Alfred crawled up in the back and called us to join him. We sat down at the back of the pickup bed and watched the world go by.

Whilst we were watching the cars and the people, I noticed that Drover had begun snapping at snowflakes. I mean, he really seemed to be getting a thrill out of it. For some reason, that irritated me.

"Why are you doing that?"

"Who me? Oh, I don't know. I never stopped to think about it."

"Well, stop and think about it. What's the purpose of it? What good's it doing?"

"Well, let's see." He thought. "I don't know."

"Think harder. If there's a purpose behind it, I want to hear it. If there's no purpose, you should quit."

"Well, okay, let me think here." He thought again. "I've got it now. Every snowflake I catch in my mouth is one that won't pile up on the street, so I guess I'm preventing snowdrifts."

76

"Preventing snowdrifts. Do you have any idea how many snowflakes you'd have to catch to prevent one snowdrift?"

"Well, let me think here. How many flakes are in a drift?"

"That depends on the size of the flakes."

"Big flakes."

"All right. Then it depends on the size of the drift."

"Big drift."

"Okay, there are a hundred and twenty-three big flakes in a big drift."

"I'll be derned, how'd you know that?"

"It's common knowledge, Drover. You just have to know your weights and measures. For example, there are five toes in a foot, one foot in a boot, and three feet in a yard. There are five yards in a city block and ten blocks weigh a ton."

"I'll swan. How many toes in a ton?"

"A hundred and twenty-three, the same number as flakes in a drift."

"How'd you come up with that?"

"Easy. You divide feet into toes, boots into feet, yards into boots, and multiply all that times four."

"How come four?"

"Because four is the only whole number between three and five."

"Huh. I hadn't thought of that. Do all numbers live in holes?"

"No. Some do but some don't. It just depends."

"Oh. Well, if all whole numbers don't live in holes, what does?"

"Prairie dogs, ground squirrels, and cotton-tail rabbits."

"How many rabbits in a hole?"

"Four."

"Now, how'd you know that?"

"I told you, Drover, four is a whole number. You're making me repeat myself."

"Well . . . I still don't understand how you can figger all that stuff in your head."

I placed a paw on his shoulder and looked him in the eyes. "The head, Drover, that's the important thing. At last you've come to the crux of the core."

"What's a crux?"

"A crux is like a small crutch, and I think that's all the time we have for weights and measures. If you have any more questions, we'll take them up at another time."

"I've still got a few."

"In the meantime, go back to snapping snowflakes. I've run the numbers on it and it appears that you might be able to prevent a snowdrift or two."

"Oh good. But I never dreamed that it could be so complicated."

"Everything's complicated, Drover. If this world was simple, dogs like you might be running it."

"That's kind of scary."

"Exactly."

Drover went back to snapping at snow-flakes, only now he had a better idea of what he was doing and why he was doing it. Heavy duty analysis has a way of bringing purpose to a guy's work.

He was snapping at snowflakes and Little Alfred and I were watching the world go by, when all of a sudden we heard a voice that came out of nowhere.

It was a loud voice, a shrill voice, an angry voice, and it said—if I can remember the exact words—it said, "Junior! Son, I'm either tied up in a gunny sack or else I've gone blind!"

# 9

# LITTLE ALFRED OPENS A PANDOWDY'S BOX

I turned to Mister Snap-At-The-Snowflakes. "Did you just say something?"

SNAP! "What?"

"I said, 'Did you just say something?' "

"I said, 'What?' "

"No, before that, something about being blind or tied up in a gunny sack?"

"Well, let's see." SNAP! "Got 'im! That snowflake won't make a drift."

"Concentrate, Drover, this could be important. Unless I'm badly mistaken, what we have here is The Case of the Mysterious Blind Man's Voice."

"Gosh." SNAP! "Got another one."

"Did you say anything about being blind?"

"I don't think so. If I said anything, it was

probably about snowflakes.'' SNAP! "Boy, this is fun.''

My interrogation of Drover was leading nowhere. I was pretty muchly convinced that he was telling the truth and that the mysterious voice hadn't been his. And it had been too low and too loud to have come from Little Alfred.

That left . . . well, nobody but ME as a suspect, and I was almost positive that . . . suddenly I noticed a gunny sack on the bed of the pickup. IT WAS MOVING!

You think I didn't let out a bark? You think the hair on my back and neck didn't stick straight up? Hey, any time I see a gunny sack moving around on the bed of a pickup . . . I mean, that ain't natural. Gunny sacks don't move around unless . . . .

Oh.

I'd almost . . . .

Let me rephrase what I just said about the so-called mysterious voice and the movable gunny sack. I wouldn't want to be quoted out of contacts.

What you supposed was a mysterious voice, coming out of nowhere, actually belonged to Wallace the Buzzard. You had probably forgotten that we had left him tied up in a gunny sack, see, and . . . .

It was the buzzard, that's the point. He had made the voice and he had caused the gunny sack to move around. I wanted to clear that little detail up before we went any further.

Just as I had suspected, Wallace the Wounded Buzzard had begun to stir in his sack. He was calling for Junior, and it appeared that he wanted out.

I looked at Little Alfred and he looked at me. "It's the buzzood!"

Heh. It had taken the boy a while to catch on. He was a little slow on the draw, but heck, he was only a kid. You have to give these kids a little time to develop their . . . .

Alfred stood up and walked over to the sack. It was wiggling around. "Do you weckon I should wet him out? Maybe the poor buzzood can't bweeve."

Uh . . . .

Letting the buzzard out of the sack didn't strike me as a real good idea, not at that particular moment. I mean, we were parked in the middle of town, right? And Slim hadn't come out of the swimming pool yet, and . . . .

No. Opening the sack was a BAD idea. There's an old saying about squeezing toothpaste out of the tube or letting a cat out of the bag or opening Pandowdy's Box or something like that, and although I can't pull it out of the vapors right this minute, it's an excellent old saying. But the point of it is that buzzards should be left in their sacks.

However, Little Alfred had a mind of his own, and he went to fiddling with the tie string on the neck of the sack. I sat and watched, shook my head, whimpered, thumped my tail against the pickup bed, did everything I could to discourage the little stinkpot from doing what he was fixing to do.

But he did it anyway.

"Drover," I said, "our little pal is fixing to open Pandowdy's Box, and once the cat's out of the bag we'll never get him back in the toothpaste tube."

He stared at me and twisted his head to the side. "What are you talking about?"

"I'm talking about a wreck."

"Oh. Was anybody hurt?" SNAP! "Got another one."

"Stand by for Battle Stations. I've got a feeling . . . ."

As soon as the cake string fell away from the neck of the sack, Wallace emerged in all his flapping, squawking, buzzard glory.

"Junior! Son, the scales have fell from my eyes and I can see the light, and, son, it's a glorious light! It will light up the night, and it will light up the darkness, and it will light up a path for the people, and the people will come to the light, and they will be enlightened by that bright and shining light!"

Little Alfred stared at the buzzard with big moon eyes. He turned to me and said, "Uh oh." And I nodded my head.

He'd done it now. He'd let the buzzard out of the bag, and that buzzard showed signs of being at least two-thirds crazy. Wallace was awake and he was talking, but he still couldn't fly and it appeared that he thought Alfred was his son Junior.

That's pretty crazy.

"Son, all these years your old daddy has lived a wasteful life and has never cared about nobody but hisself and his next meal, but today, on this very spot and at this very moment, your old daddy has seen the light and has decided . . . to run for public office!"

That caught Drover's attention, and all at once he quit snapping at snowflakes. His head came around real slow.

"Did you hear what I just heard?"

"I heard it, Drover. Now ask me if I believe it."

"Do you believe it?"

"Negative."

"Me too."

Little Alfred must have realized that he'd made a mistake, because he made a grab at the buzzard. But buzzards, even those that are wounded and dingy in the head, are big birds, and it takes more than a four-year-old boy to get one under control.

For his efforts, Little Alfred got thrashed by Wallace's wings. "Unhand me, son, this world of darkness and trouble is waiting for the news of my campaign for public office!"

Wallace hopped and waddled his way toward the rear of the pickup bed. Drover and I happened to be in his path.

"You can stop right there, Wallace," I said. "This thing has gone . . . ."

He stuck his ugly beak into my face. "Dog, have you ever been throwed up on by a big, mean buzzard?"

"Uh . . . no sir, can't say as I have."

"Step aside before you do."

"Yes sir."

I stepped aside. Little Drover scrambled out of the way and took cover behind me. Wallace went to the back end of the pickup and called to a group of town dogs who happened to be walking past.

The thought crossed my mind that he shouldn't have done that. Those dogs were big and scruffy, and looked about half-mean.

"Y'all come over here! That's right, come on over and hear this important announcement which I'm a-fixing to make, for you see, this is a very important day in the history of this town and this world!"

The dogs exchanged glances, smirked at each other, and came rumbling over. Uh oh. It was Buster and Muggs and the other two hoodlums.

"Wallace," I said, "I think you're about to . . . ."

"You hush up, pooch! You'll never learn nuthin' in this life as long as your mouth stays open."

"You'd better take your own advice, is my advice to you."

"I never take advice from a dog." He turned back to the dogs who had gathered down below. "It gives me great pleasure, indeed GREAT pleasure to make the following public announcement to all the public and all the people and all the world, for I have seen the light and have made the most important decision of my life and your life."

There was a moment of silence. Wallace puffed himself up, threw back his head, and went on.

"In this very place, at this very moment of this very day, after long years of silence on the many important issues of the times, I have decided to answer the call of my many, many friends and supporters . . . and run for the office of His Feathered Majesty."

Down below the thugs stared at him with open mouths. There was a moment of stunned silence. Then they all burst out laughing, and

Buster turned to Muggs. "Say, who is this guy?"

"I don't know, Boss, but he looks like a turkey to me, and we ain't got no Christmas turkey yet."

"Yeah, I see what you mean. Turkey for Christmas would be all right, wouldn't it, Muggsie?"

"Har har, yeah, sure would, and it was my idea too, wasn't it, Boss, huh, wasn't it, tell the truth?"

"Shat up, Muggs."

Wallace went on with his speech.

"Experience: that's what I bring to this contest, friends and neighbors. Nobody in this race has more feathers than Wallace the Buzzard. I was born with feathers. I've wore 'em all my life, and I plan to leave this old world with my feathers on.

"Where do I stand on the issues? I stand right here, and you have my solemn pledge that I will throw up on all ninnies that don't vote the right way. I'm for cleaning the dead rabbits off these highways. I'm for adequate moisture. And you want to know what I'm against?"

From down below there was a chorus of

"NO!". That didn't faze old Wallace. He was on a roll.

"I'm against elm beetles! Elect me to this great office and I will, personally and single-handedly, lead a moral crusade against these corrupt agents who are killin' our beautiful elm trees along the creek!

"That's my promise and that's my pledge to you on this very day as I stand before you, a candidate for public office. If elected, I will pass a law against elm beetles!"

The thugs were getting restless, and I could see that they had bad things in mind for a certain buzzard. Little Alfred must have seen it too. He climbed off the pickup bed and headed for the Swimming Pool Hall as fast as his little legs would carry him.

Not a bad idea, because I had a feeling that things were about to get out of hand.

# 10

# THE BIG SHOWDOWN
# WITH BUGGS
# AND MUSTER

I tried to warn the buzzard.

"Uh, Wallace, if I were you I think I'd button my beak and crawl into the first gunny sack I could find. You're getting those dogs stirred up."

"Heh? Of course I'm gettin' 'em stirred up. I want 'em stirred up! The trouble with this country right now is that nobody's stirred up about this elm beetle problem."

"Yeah, well, I don't think those dogs give a rip about the elm beetle problem. They think you're a turkey, and they're considering you as a candidate for Christmas dinner."

"Who called me a turkey! Junior! Where'd

he go? Son, they're callin' me a turkey, where'd that boy go, just when you need him most he disappears, Junior!" He craned his neck and studied the dogs on the street. "Y'all seen any signs of Junior? Tell Junior to report here at once, somebody just called me a turkey and Junior needs to know about that!"

Buster grinned. "Oh yeah? Let me tell you something, Pops. I called you a turkey because you ARE a turkey, and me and my boys have this terrible appetite for turkey, don't we, Muggs?"

Muggs was bouncing up and down. "Yeah, har har, we sure do, Boss, and I think I know what we're fixing to do about it too, har har."

The time had come for me to get involved, even though I didn't want to. I went to the back of the pickup, pushed Wallace aside, and spoke to the mob.

"Boys, you're making a big mistake here. Wallace may look like a turkey and he may act like a turkey, but he ain't a turkey. He's a turkey *buzzard,* and you wouldn't want to eat him for Christmas dinner."

Down below, Buster's eyes narrowed and he turned to Muggs. "Say, Muggsie, haven't we seen this wise guy somewhere before?"

"Yeah, we sure have, Boss, out at that

ranch. He's the jerk that made me laugh at stupid jokes.''

''Oh yeah, the Head of Ranch Security.''

''Yeah, har har, only he ain't got no ranch now and he's in town—our town, har har.''

''I think you're right, Muggsie.'' Buster turned back to me and took a step in my direction. ''Let me tell you something, pal. Me and my boys are hungry, see? And when we get hungry, we're extra mean. And if you want to keep on being the Head of Ranch Security, you'd better step aside and mind your own business, see?''

''I think you missed the point, Buster.''

''It's Mister Buster to you, pal.''

''Yeah,'' said Muggs, ''it's Mister Buster to you, buster, or we'll bust you right in the mouth, won't we, Boss?''

''That's right, Muggsie. You've got a way with the words.''

I went on. ''As I was saying, this guy's a buzzard, not a turkey.''

''Oh yeah?'' Buster grinned. ''If he's a buzzard, what's he doing in town, huh? Buzzards don't come to town, pal, but turkeys do.''

''That's right, Boss, you sure told him, har har har! We know a turkey when we see one, he can't fool us.''

I turned to the buzzard. "Wallace, can you fly?"

"Heh? Where's a fly? Show me a fly! Where there's a fly, there's something good to eat."

"I said, *can you fly*?"

"Oh. You mean with my wings? No, I cain't fly, my wings ain't a-workin'. No, I cain't fly, no, absolutely not."

"In that case, I'd advise you to start thinking about making a run for it."

"Heh? Run? Buzzards don't run, it goes against all our principles. If we cain't fly, we just stay home."

"Well, if you don't make a run for it, those dogs down there are going to make a turkey sandwich out of you."

"No, I never eat turkey, just rabbits and skunks and things on the side of the road."

Talking to Wallace was hopeless. That wreck had wrecked what little mind he'd had to start with, and now it was up to me and Drover to save him from the mob.

"Drover, move on up here with me. It's time for us to stand toe-to-toe and assume Battle Stations."

"Hank, this old leg of mine is sure giving me fits all of a sudden."

"Battle Stations, Drover, and that's a direct order!"

"Oh my leg!" He came limping over and joined me at the back of the pickup. He looked down at the thugs and almost fainted. "Oh my gosh, don't say anything to make 'em mad, Hank!"

Buster and Muggs saw Drover there beside me and started laughing. Then Buster said, "What is this, pal? Are we choosing up sides for a fight or something?"

"You might say that. This buzzard's lost his marbles and he's under my protection. Now, you boys go on about your business and we'll go on about ours. Scram."

Muggsie's ears shot up. "Hey Boss, the jerk said for us to scram! I heard it with my own eyes!"

"Yeah, I heard what he said. Okay, boys, we ain't had a good riot around here in a couple of days. I think it's time we started one."

Muggsie was hopping up and down again. "Yeah, right! Just say the word, Boss, I'll teach that jerk a lesson he won't forget!"

Buster leered up at me. "Last chance, pal. I ain't sure I can hold my boys back any longer, see? We're coming up there to get our turkey dinner, and if you stay where you're at we'll make cranberry sauce out of you and your sawed-off friend.''

Drover let out a gasp. "Hank, oh my gosh, did you hear that? Help, murder!"

"Stand your ground, Drover. The reputation of our ranch is at stake here."

"My LIFE is at stake here, and I think this old leg's about to give out, help, Mayday!"

"Don't bite until you see the whites of their eyes, Drover! Stand by for hand-to-hand combat!"

"Oh, my leg!"

"All right, boys," Buster shouted, "this is the moment you've been waiting for. Stand by to hit the beach! Okay, Muggs, get 'em!"

Muggs was the first to test our defense perimeter. He made a lunge and landed on the edge of the pickup bed. I met him there with teeth, paws, and claws—also Extra Heavy Duty Barking. I punched him right on the end of his bulldog nose and sent him flying back to his boss.

"Sorry about that, Muggsie, but you were tracking snow on my pickup. Who's next? Come on, boys, don't quit now, I'm just getting warmed up."

"Hank, don't say that!" Drover squeaked.

"They might believe you."

"Okay, smart guy," said Buster, glaring up at me. "You've asked for it, and now you'll get it."

"Yeah, jerk," said Muggs, "you shouldn't have done that, you just shouldn't ought to have done that, 'cause now you're in deep trouble."

I ran my eyes over the faces in the mob. I knew that they were fixing to attack the pickup in force, and I knew that when they did, I wouldn't be able to fight them off.

I turned to my assistant—who was lying on the pickup bed with his paws over his eyes. "Get up, Drover, and listen carefully to my instructions. When they attack, bite that buzzard on the tail feathers and make him run. I'll fight 'em off as long as I can, and you guys try to find a place to hide."

"I hear that!"

"And Drover," I looked down at the little mutt, perhaps for the last time, "if I don't make it back from this mission, take care of the ranch."

"I sure will, Hank, if this old leg stays under me. Come on, Wallace, we've got to run for our lives!"

"Heh? Run? Son, let me tell you something

about buzzards and running. If we cain't fly . . . ."

Drover opened his jaws and crunched Wallace on the tail section, gave him quite a shock. He squawked, flapped his wings, hopped up in the air, and went over the side. Drover bailed out right behind him.

That was the last I saw of them for a while, because at that very moment I heard four double-tough town dogs coming after me from down below. I turned and faced the attack with a smile that was somewhat forced.

"Come on, boys. You've heard of the Alamo? Well, it's Alamo time. Remember the Alamo, charge, bonzai!"

I took the first one, thrashed him good, and sent him flying off the back end. Then I went after the second one, just by George hammered him, sent him over the side.

But that was about the end of the good part. Muggs swooped in on me from behind, put a fang lock on the back of my neck, and let me tell you about Muggsie's jaws. What he lacked in brainpower he more than made up for in jawpower.

I couldn't shake loose, see, and while he held me from behind, Buster swaggered up and started working me over with paws and claws.

"Here's what happens to jerks that stand in the way of our turkey dinner."

And he proceeded to clean house on my nose and face, especially my nose. It hurt! I gave it my best shot, fellers, but by that time the whole bunch had dog-piled me and I was getting it from all directions.

Then I heard Muggsie's voice. "Hey Boss, the turkey's gone!"

"Huh, what? The turkey's . . . why you idiot, you let our turkey dinner get away!"

"It wasn't me, Boss, honest. It was the other guys."

"You're all idiots! What do you think we're doing up here? We're fighting for our turkey dinner, you dummies!"

"Yeah, Boss, but you said . . . ."

"Shat up. Where'd he go? Find the turkey! Come on, boys, never mind the Head of Ranch Security. We'll take care of him some other time. After the turkey!"

And with that, the hoodlums went flying over the side of the pickup, leaving me behind—crippled, bruised, bloodied, and humiliated.

But not quite beaten.

CHAPTER

# 11

# OH, IT WAS SANTIE CLAUS, NOT SANDY CLOTHES

I scraped myself off the pickup bed and checked out all my various bodily parts for damage. I found plenty of it, but lucky for me, it was of the non-permanent variety.

After walking around and limbering up my equipment, I figgered I had better make my way to the Combat Zone. If Buster and his hoodlum friends found Wallace before I did, my pal Junior the Buzzard was likely to get orphaned for Christmas.

I dived off the pickup and began sniffing the snow.

The trail led off to the north, towards the big white grain elevator that rose above the railroad tracks at the north end of town. I locked in on the scent, put my smellatory transponders on automatic, and went zooming up the street.

While zooming up the street, I began to notice the crowd of people who had gathered on the sidewalks on both sides. Some of them were pointing at me, others laughing and clapping their hands.

It seems that I had attracted a crowd. I mean, people had come from miles around and lined both sides of Main Street to see me do my stuff. Pretty impressive, huh?

It took double the usual amount of concentration for me to concentrate on my business. I mean, no matter how many times you've performed before an adoring crowd, it's hard to resist—well—prancing, showing off, throwing in a few extra tricks, performing the little flourishes that are sure to bring squeals of delight from the ladies, and so forth.

A guy gets to watching the crowd, see, and especially the ladies, and you know Twitchell had more than its fair share of fine-looking lady dogs, and my concentration slipped just a tad, and before I knew it . . . .

HUH? I found myself surrounded by Buster and his gang. I glanced around and took a quick reading of my position. It appeared that I had reached the north end of Main Street, in the very middle of a large crowd of people. Nearby was a . . . what was that thing?

A *sleigh?* With wheels under it instead of runners? Pulled by a paint horse? And sitting in the sleigh was a very suspicious-looking man with a LONG WHITE BEARD, AND WEARING A RED AND WHITE SUIT!

G.L. Holmes

Little Alfred was standing beside the sleigh, and a big crowd of people were gathered around him, and hunkered down underneath the sleigh was Wallace the Buzzard.

And right beside him, shivering in the snow, was Drover.

The pieces of the puzzle were beginning to fall into place. This crowd had gathered to cheer me on as I fought against tremendous odds to defend a helpless, wounded, partially-crazy old buzzard against tremendous odds and a pack of town dogs.

The one piece of the puzzle that DIDN'T fall into place was: who was this strange guy in the beard and red suit? I didn't know, but it didn't much matter anyway. My work was cut out for me. These people had come to watch me do my stuff and, by George, I was ready to give 'em their money's worth.

I turned to Buster. "And so, Buster, it seems that we meet again."

"Yeah, so it seems. Where's my turkey dinner, smart guy, and get right to the point."

I was about to give him a witty, really devastating reply, when Muggs blundered into the conversation.

"Hey Boss, the turkey's under that thing over there with the horse!"

Buster narrowed his eyes, looked toward the sleigh or whatever it was, and a wicked grin spread across his mouth. "You're right, Muggs. Okay, boys, this is it. We've got our bird cornered. Spread out and . . . ."

"Hold it right there, halt, stop! The first dog that moves will have to answer to me."

Buster snorted at that. "Answer to you! Ha! Out of the way, cowdog, before I have to sweep the street with your carcass. Get the turkey, boys!"

They made a rush for the sleigh. By running backwards at full speed (pretty nifty trick right there), I was able to stay in front of them and cut off their attack, and when we reached the sleigh at the same moment, I established a do-or-die position of defense and launched myself into the middle of them.

Pretty risky, huh? Sure it was, but hey, that's what my fans had come to see, right? Maybe I wouldn't have done that without the support of hundreds of supporters, but . . . .

Well, several things happened right away. Me and Buster met head-on in a fight to the bitter end. We slashed and clawed and snarled, climbed each other until we couldn't climb any more, came back down, and went rolling through the snow.

Behind me, I could hear Drover cheering me on. "Git 'im, Hankie, git 'im! Knock his eye out! Punch him in the nose!"

As I say, we went rolling through the snow—right between the legs of the horse. A lot of horses will spook when a dogfight breaks out between their legs, don't you see, and this horse was one of those. He spooked.

The next thing that happened was that Muggs got after Wallace, who came squawking and flapping out from under the sleigh. Right behind him came Muggs, barking and snapping.

Behind Muggs came Little Alfred, shouting, "Weeve that buzzood awone, you naughty dog!" And behind Little Alfred came three or four men from the crowd, shouting and waving their arms.

They ran right in front of the horse, who had already begun to snort and pitch. And fellers, when he saw that buzzard flapping through the snow he made a real serious attempt to kick us dogs into the next county and haul that sleigh down to the Gulf of Mexico.

Above it all, I could hear the guy with the white beard, yelling, "Whoa, Flower, easy, boy!"

Things were looking pretty grim, seemed to

me, when all at once who should come running out of the crowd but Slim. He went to the horse's head, threw his right elbow over the pony's neck, and grabbed an ear in each hand.

The horse was rearing up so hard that he lifted old Slim off the ground several times, but Slim held on and shouted, "Somebody grab that buzzard before he gets us all killed!"

Three grown men took after Wallace, chased him around in circles while the crowd pushed forward, laughing and cheering them on.

At last they captured Wallace just about the time that Slim had talked Flower out of leaving the country. A cheer went up from the crowd. It was hard to tell if they were cheering Slim, the guys who had collared Wallace, or me.

I guess we had all made our little contributions, although mine wasn't so little.

So there you are. They were cheering for me.

Two men stepped forward and shook Slim's hand and thanked him for saving . . . oh . . . Santie Claus. So that's who that guy . . . they were trying to have a parade for this guy Santie Claus, see, and . . . okay.

You thought his name was Sandy Clothes? Nope. Santie Claus.

At any rate, one of the men said, "What should we do with this buzzard? He can't fly, and we don't have any idea how he got here in town."

It seemed to me that Slim's face turned a deep shade of red, and he said, "Well, we're fixing to head back to the ranch. I guess I could haul him out to the country and turn him a-loose."

Little Alfred was standing beside Slim and started to say something, but he never got past the second word because all at once he had Slim's big gloved hand over his mouth.

"Would you mind?" said the man. "That would sure be nice, and then maybe we can get this dadgum parade started."

The crowd cheered. Several men slapped old Slim on the back, and they gave him the buzzard. Even Santie Claus himself stepped down and shook Slim's hand.

I still didn't like the looks of that Santie Claus guy, and as he passed I bristled up and growled at him. You know what he said? "Buzz off, pooch, or I'll give you a Tony Lama sandwich."

Seemed kind of unfriendly to me.

Well, Slim called us dogs and Little Alfred, and he pushed a path through the crowd towards the pickup. As I was leaving, I happened to pass Buster. He'd been kicked and stepped on by the horse, and had gotten several good scoldings from people in the crowd. I gave him a smirk and said, "Let this be a lesson to you, Buster. Chinners never win and cheaters never weep."

"Oh yeah? Well, so's yer old man. We'll meet again, pal, and if you ever set foot in this town again . . . ."

At that moment, Santie Claus stepped on Buster's tail and booted him out of the way. That was good enough for me. We marched to our pickup and headed back to the country.

CHAPTER

# 12

# ALL'S SWELL THAT ENDS SWELL

Slim seemed pretty anxious to get out of town. He didn't say a word until we had passed the Waterhole and were out on the flat open country south of town.

Then he turned an evil eye on the three of us—me, Drover, and Little Alfred.

"I don't know which one of you knotheads turned that buzzard a-loose in town, but I AIN'T amused. He goes back out into the snow, where he came from. I've had about enough of pets for one day."

Little Alfred hung his head and stuck out his lower lip. "But Swim, it's Cwismas Eve."

"Son, a famous man once had this to say about Christmas Eve: 'Bah and humbug!' And if he'd had two dogs, a kid, and a buzzard,

111

he'd have said worse than that. The buzzard goes."

Well, Slim's heart had certainly turned cold, which wasn't too surprising since the snow and wind and cold air were coming through what used to be the windshield and we were all about to freeze.

Little Alfred sat back in the seat and looked out the window at the snow-covered wheat-fields that stretched as far as the eye could see. It was kind of a sad moment, to tell you the truth.

Even I felt a little sad. Wallace probably didn't deserve our sympathy, but still . . . throwing a wounded animal out into the snow on Christmas Eve . . . that was a pretty harsh sentence.

All at once, Little Alfred started singing a song he'd learned in Sunday school. It went like this:

Oh wittle town of Beffweeham, how still
    we see thee wie.
Above thy deep and dweemwess sweep,
    the siwent stars go by.
Yet in thy dark stweets shineth the
    evoowasting wight.
The hopes and fee-ohs of all the yee-ohs
Are met in thee tonight.

While the boy sang, Drover and I thumped our tails against the cold seat and beamed mournful stares at Cold-Hearted Slim.

When we came to the spot in the road where we'd run into Wallace that morning, Slim slowed down, put his foot on the brake . . . and kept on going.

All he said was, "You knotheads."

We followed the creek road all the way down to the place where you turn off to go to Slim's house. We turned, rumbled over the cattle guard, drove through his horse pasture, and pulled up in front of his house.

He killed the motor and turned to us. "We'll take your buzzard inside and thaw him out by the fire. But I ain't spending the night with a buzzard, so when he gets thawed out we're going to move him down to the calf shed. That's my best offer, Christmas or no Christmas."

"Okay, Swim. And I won't tell anybody why we missed the pawade. It's a secwet."

"It *better* be a secret."

We piled out of the pickup. Slim gathered up a load of wood, went inside, and built a fire in the stove. Then he went outside and came back with the gunny sack. He didn't take Wallace out of the sack, which was probably a smart idea, but laid him and the sack out in front of the fire.

While Slim wrapped up Sally May and Miss Viola's presents in grocery sacks, we gathered around the stove and waited to see if Wallace would snap out of it. He didn't move or make a sound.

The stove warmed up and the chill went out of the house. We waited. Then the gunny sack moved, just a little bit. Then it moved a whole bunch.

Slim stopped wrapping and watched. We all watched. The next thing we knew, the sack was jumping around on the floor and Old Wallace was raising a fuss.

"Let me out of this dad-blamed . . . , open up this sack this very minute and let me . . . , Junior, where are you, son? They've got me locked up in a burlap poke, son, and . . . y'all just better let me out of this sack or I'll show you how much damage an angry buzzard can do, is what's fixin' to happen if y'all don't."

Slim laid down his scissors and nodded his head. "I think the patient has pulled through. Now he goes to the calf shed."

He pulled on his coat and overshoes and carried Wallace, still in the sack, down to the calf shed. Drover, Little Alfred, and I followed.

Slim dragged up a couple of bales of prairie hay and made a little bed for the buzzard.

Then he untied the sack and poured Wallace out on the hay. Anybody who had expected Wallace to come out in a sweet and cheerful mood would have been disappointed, because he came out mad—in other words, the same old reprobate buzzard we'd always known.

Slim wanted no part of an angry buzzard, and once he'd dumped Wallace out on the hay he made a quick retreat back to the house to finish wrapping his presents.

Just as he rounded the corner of the house and disappeared from view we heard a thump on the tin roof, and a moment later Junior came flapping and crashing down beside us.

He was grinning from ear to ear, although buzzards don't exactly have . . . he had a big grin spread from one side of his beak to the other. In other words, he was one happy buzzard.

"Oh P-p-pa, y-you're alive and s-s-s-s-safe! I was s-s-so w-w-worried and s-s-s-sad!"

He rushed to the old man and wrapped him up in a big hug with his wings.

"Here, git back, what's all this . . . of course I'm alive and safe, what did you expect, but no thanks at all to these ninnies, they had me tied up in a burlap poke, I liked to have froze to death and suffocated in that thang!"

Junior told him the whole story, about how he'd crashed through the windshield of the pickup and we'd taken pity on him and saved his life, the whole story.

Do you think the old man was grateful? No sir. He didn't remember any of it.

"Junior, that is without a doubt the most outrageous, ridiculous, windy tale I ever heard. I did not run into no pickup, I have never ever in my whole life been inside a town and never will, and I want to know right this minute how I got this knot on the top of my head!"

"S-s-s-see? Y-you d-d-did run into the p-p-p-p-p-p . . . uh, truck, and that's h-h-how y-you g-g-g-got the knot, got the knot. And sh-sh-shame on y-you for t-t-talking so m-m-mean to the v-v-v-very ones who s-s-saved your l-l-l-l-l-l-l . . . skin. Sh-shame on y-y-you!

Wallace's head rose in the air. "Junior! Did you just say shame on me?"

"Y-y-yeah. And sh-shame on y-y-you again."

"I thought that's what you said."

116

"It's g-good m-manners to th-th-thank your f-f-f-friends."

"Says who?"

"Emily P-p-p-p-post, the g-good m-m-manners l-lady."

"Son, have I told you lately what I think of Emily Post and her good manners? Listen to this."

Wallace crossed his wings in front of his chest and scowled and sang a song. Here's how it went.

### A Pox, A Pox On Emily Post

You tell me of this etiquette and of this
    savoir-faire
But I no speak-a French, son, and I don't
    even care.
'Cause God made me a buzzard, uncouth
    and loud and free,
And all this stuff on etiquette, it cuts no ice
    with me.

    A pox, a pox on Emily Post,
    I thumb my nose at Emily's ghost,
    I'll never be Miss Emily's host
    She cuts no ice with me.

Now let's just take a closer look at old Miss
   Emily's name.
Post is what they called her, and manners
   were her game.
Out here they have a use for posts, they
   plant 'em in the ground.
A barbed wire fence with Emily posts? I'll
   pass that word around!

   A pox, a pox on Emily Post,
   I thumb my nose at Emily's ghost,
   I'll never be Miss Emily's host
   So pass that word around.

No self-respecting buzzard has time for
   building couth.
We've got no use for manners, and that's
   the gospel truth.
So take your please and thank you and
   stick 'em in your ear.
The Devil can roast Miss Emily Post and I
   will raise a cheer.

   A pox, a pox on Emily Post,
   I thumb my nose at Emily's ghost,
   I'll never be Miss Emily's host
   And I will raise a cheer.

When he'd finished the song, Old Man Wallace seemed right proud of himself. "There! So take your please and thank you and stick 'em in your ear."

Junior looked at me and shrugged. "H-h-he sure h-hates to s-s-say th-th-thank you, d-d-don't he?"

"So it seems, Junior, but that's okay. Nobody around here cares what he thinks anyway."

"See?" yelled Wallace. "I knew they didn't really care, it was all just a big show!"

Junior's head swung back to the old man. "P-p-pa?"

"What!"

"Sh-sh-shut u-u-up."

The old buzzard's beak fell open, and the rest of us stared at Junior. By George, it had taken him a lot of years to get those two simple words out of his beak, but he'd finally done it.

Well, maybe Old Man Wallace didn't have anything to be thankful for, but I did. Heck, I had four good legs, two ears, two eyes, and a tail. I was out of the wind and the snow. I had friends. I had enough Co-op dog food to keep myself running.

And besides all that, it was Christmas Eve—

the only Christmas Eve we were going to have that year. It would have been a real shame to let the evening pass without us singing at least one Christmas carol.

So, before we all broke up and went our separate ways, I proposed that we do just that.

And you know what? We did, me and Junior and Drover and Little Alfred. Old Man Wallace refused to sing, which was okay because too many buzzards can ruin a Christmas carol.

Well, it was a great occasion and pretty outstanding singing too. When we were done, Junior said they needed to get back to their roost.

"Well, Junior, it was fun. Goodbye and I hope you have a wonderful Christmas."

"Th-thanks, and M-m-merry Christmas to y-y-you t-t-too."

G.L.Holmes

"Thanks, Junior. And Merry Christmas to you too, Wallace, even though you don't deserve it."

"That's right and I'm proud of it, Christmas is just for ninnies and children, and my last word on the subject is phooey on Christmas. Goodbye and good riddance."

And with that, they flew away into the snowy sky. Seemed to me that we had us a pretty swell ending for the story, and as they say, all's swell that ends swell, so let's just quit.

Hazelwood Elementary School
11815 S.E. 304th St.
Auburn, WA 98002